every leaf
a hallelujah

Also by Ben Okri

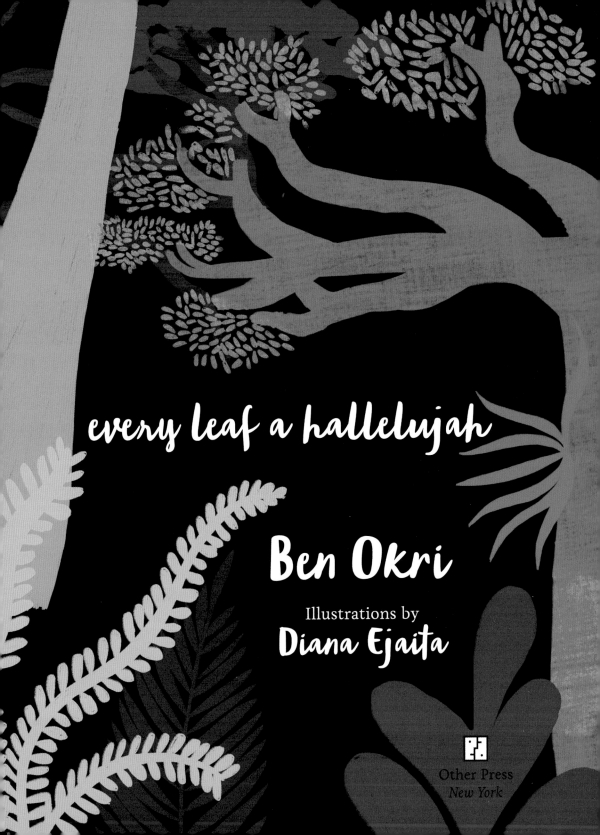

every leaf a hallelujah

Ben Okri

Illustrations by
Diana Ejaita

Other Press
New York

First published in the UK in 2021 by Head of Zeus Ltd
Text © Ben Okri, 2021
Illustrations © Diana Ejaita, 2021

Production editor: Yvonne E. Cárdenas
Text designer: Jessie Price

1 3 5 7 9 10 8 6 4 2

Library of Congress Cataloging-in-Publication Data
Names: Okri, Ben, author. | Ejaita, Diana, illustrator.
Title: Every leaf a hallelujah / Ben Okri ; illustrations by Diana Ejaita.
Description: New York : Other Press, [2022]
Identifiers: LCCN 2021042598 (print) | LCCN 2021042599 (ebook) |
ISBN 9781635422702 (hardcover) | ISBN 9781635422719 (ebook)
Subjects: CYAC: Fairy tales. | Quests (Expeditions)—Fiction. |
Forests and forestry—Fiction. | Ecology—Fiction. |
Trees—Fiction. | LCGFT: Fairy tales. | Ecofiction.
Classification: LCC PZ7.1.O448 Ev 2022 (print) | LCC PZ7.1.O448 (ebook) |
DDC [E—dc23
LC record available at https://lccn.loc.gov/2021042598
LC ebook record available at https://lccn.loc.gov/2021042599

Dear Reader

When I was young I thought the beauty of the forest would last for ever. Now I'm not so sure. Certain grown-ups, who have forgotten their childhoods and who care more about money than nature, are destroying the forests.

When I was a child I knew that trees were more important than money. Trees make us happy. Can you imagine a world without them? That's why I wrote this story. If trees could write, they would tell you the story themselves. We can only hear their stories when we befriend them.

If we look after them, they will look after us. I hope you love trees. They are not what they seem. They are magic and they touch our lives with magic too.

Ben Okri
London

One day a little girl called Mangoshi went into the forest on an errand and got lost. As she tried to make her way back home she found herself among strange-looking trees. Something about the trees worried her at first. They seemed to be whispering. She was not sure where the sound was coming from. It sounded like a river nearby, like the murmur of insects, but no insects ever sounded like this. It came from high up among the treetops and low down among the lower branches. Then sometimes it sounded among the roots. She pressed her ear to the earth and thought she heard the roots whispering. All this puzzled her. She had to get back soon, for it was getting dark. Her parents would start to worry about her.

She had been sent on an errand into the forest to pluck a special flower that grows on the oldest tree. The flower was meant to help heal her mother's illness. The journey had been simple. She had found the flower, but on the way back the paths had seemed to multiply and become confusing. Mangoshi did not know which one to take because a strange mist obscured the familiar path. Then it was as if the forest itself was trying to confuse her, for every path she took led her deeper into the forest where she saw trees she had never seen before.

They were majestic trees, tall and vast. They looked hundreds of years old. It occurred to her that there was something sad about the trees. At the same moment she felt the sadness Mangoshi began to hear the murmurs. The mist that obscured the paths settled on her, preventing her from seeing anything.

While she wandered about in the new darkness her outstretched arms came to rest on the trunk of a tree. She stopped and sat down, too tired to go any further. She rested her back on the tree and fell into a light slumber.

She hadn't been asleep long when the murmurs she had been hearing became voices. There were deep old voices, and strong voices, and small lovely ones. They were all talking at the same time, surprised that they had at last found someone who could hear them.

"You are all talking at once," Mangoshi said, "and I can't understand you."

The voices fell silent. Perhaps they had never heard a human voice address them before.

"Let the eldest among you speak first," Mangoshi said, "and then I want to hear what each of you has to say."

The trees remained silent.

"Why don't you speak? You were all speaking at once a moment ago."

Still they were silent. Their silence was very strange to Mangoshi, stranger than their speaking all at once. Then she realized, after a while, that there was a reason for their silence.

They wanted her to be aware of what they were doing. Moments later, when she noticed what it was, it almost frightened her.

The trees had moved closer.
They had clustered round her.

The small trees were
in front and the larger
trees were behind.

The gigantic
obeches and mahoganies
leant over the others, so that their
tops looked down at the girl as if
with faces and eyes. It seemed as if the
whole forest had gathered round her, in
a dense circle, like elders at a tribal meeting.
She became aware of so many personalities: stern
old irokos that never laughed, solid obeches with
their proverbial air, bright young flame trees
with lively senses of humor, growing jacarandas
with chattering branches, very ancient baobabs
that were economical in their
movements and seemed to
pour out wisdom. There
were trees that liked
talking and ones that had
the gift of listening. They
all crowded round her and
were fascinated by her presence

among them.
But for a long
time they did
not say anything.

Then at last one of
them, a lively young
jacaranda, very sensitive
and curious, said:

"We should ask her."

"Not yet," replied
another tree.

"She isn't ready,"
said a third.

"It would be asking too much of her," said a
fourth.

"I agree," piped up a fifth. "Can't you see that
she is quite young?"

"All the better," said a sixth, a deep-voiced
obeche. "It is the young who can
understand."

"I think we should wait," said a seventh tree, who sounded very old and wise. "Let's wait and see what she's made of. It has to be the right person. It will be wasted if she's not the right person."

"She is the right person. See how she looks at us," said one who had spoken before.

"I think you're right. She can hear us, can

understand us. That's already a lot."

"Still, let's wait. We've waited this long. A bit longer won't make any difference."

This older, wiser voice seemed to decide for the rest of them. They fell silent, but still crowding round her and looking at her with wonder. She looked back at them and they seemed to her like people she knew, people from the village, people she had heard about. She was not sure why she had this feeling. They continued in their silence. At last she said:

"What is it you're waiting for?"

The trees said nothing.

"Why am I not ready? Ready for what?"

The trees stayed silent.

"I can't stay here forever. I've got to go home. My parents will be thinking something has happened to me by now."

She began to get up and the trees returned, with a swishing sound, to their original positions. They were no longer bent over her. They no longer seemed like people that she knew. They now seemed only like trees.

"Maybe it was a dream. Maybe I only imagined them talking. How silly of me," Mangoshi said aloud to herself.

Then she looked for the way back home. The path became clear and she followed it through the forest, listening to the sound of the birds and the murmur of leaves when the wind rushed past. At last she saw the rooftops of the village.

She saw people talking and
heard the noises of people in their
kitchens preparing dinner.
The fragrance of the stews made
her hurry a little. Darkness had
come over the forest. If she had
stayed in there a moment longer
she might not have found her
way home.

Her parents had been worried about her and they were relieved to see her. It was only when they asked her about the flower she was sent to pick, that she realized she didn't have it. She must have lost it somewhere in the mist. Her parents were sad she had lost it, but were happier to have their daughter back home safe and well. She ate her dinner and listened to a story her mother told her. It was the story of a hunter's strange experience in the forest. The story was so fascinating that she fell into the story and found herself talking with the hunter and wandering about in the forest. Then she was in bed. Before she fell asleep she remembered what the trees had said about her not being ready. She thought about it a lot before she drifted off.

The next day
Mangoshi was anxious to
go back to the forest. But she
had lots to do, many errands to run. It was early
in the evening, before dinner, that she found
time to play. She set out for the forest, taking
the route she had taken before. But as
she went in, the paths multiplied again and
she couldn't remember where she had gone
or where she had heard the trees talking.
She got a bit lost. The evening got darker.
She made a real effort to remember her
way home and was grateful when she
found it.

Over the next couple of days Mangoshi
did not go back to the forest. She was even
beginning to forget her experience there when
one night she heard something scratching at her
window. She went to the window, looked out,
and saw nothing but the leaves of the tree near
their house. Back in bed she was falling asleep
when she heard a whisper.

"We are waiting for you," a voice said.

Mangoshi was very sleepy. She wanted to get
up and see who was at the window, but sleep,
like a dark current, was sweeping her deeper
into its world.

"Come before it's too late," the voice
whispered, with more urgency.

Mangoshi wished she could get up.
Someone needed her. But she had crossed
over into the land of sleep and the voice
came from very far away.

"Are you ready?" it whispered,

but now it sounded as if it was coming from
the other side of the world.

Soon Mangoshi was fast asleep.

In the morning she had
only a dim memory of the voice. She went to
school, and learnt many things, and came home,
and helped her mother around the house.

A whole year passed in this way.

Mangoshi forgot about the forest. She forgot
about her strange experience with the trees. And
she forgot about the voice that was calling her
that night.

But as time passed she noticed small changes
in their lives. The harvests grew poorer and they
had less to eat. Strange animals appeared in the
village. It became very hot in the daytime. Then
people began falling ill and no one knew where
the illness came from.

Mangoshi's mother grew weaker and weaker.
Once again, the wise man of the village said

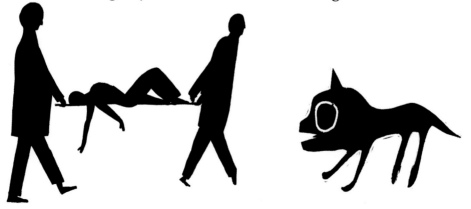

that only the special flower
which lived in the heart of
the forest could cure her, the same
flower that Mangoshi had failed to bring
back the year before. Her parents realized that
they had sent her too early last year and they
should have consulted with the wise man
before she set off.

It was decided this time that she would go early in the evening, the right time for plucking such a magical flower. But before she set off, her father sat her down.

"Mangoshi," he said, "there is a special reason why we are allowing you to go. Only a girl of seven years old can find this flower. No one else can do it. If you find it you will save not only your mother, but the whole village. Do you know what this means?"

Mangoshi nodded. She did not know what it meant, but the fact that her father felt it necessary to talk to her like this meant it was important. He had never spoken to her like this before.

"The whole village is counting on you. I would come with you but they say that you must go alone. If anyone comes with you the power of the medicine will weaken. It is your courage that makes it strong. Do you want to do this?"

"Yes, Daddy," she said.

Her father had tears in his eyes.

"I would not ask this of you, but they say you are the only one who can do this."

"Who says this?"

"The wise people who know about these things." Her father paused and looked at her. "You are going to the forest. You have been there before. The flower will be harder to find this time."

"Why?"

"You will see for yourself. The world has changed. We are all in trouble."

"Why?"

"You will see why. Human beings have not been good to the earth. But you will see." He paused again. "The forest is not the same forest you went to before. If you get lost there, if it's difficult to find your way back, there is only one thing to remember. If you bring back the flower, the flower will save the village. And if you save the village, the village will save the forest. I would like to give you a spell to help you come back safely, but I have been told not to give you a spell. It will weaken the force of the flower. They say you must do everything on your own. You

must make your own spell by yourself. You must find the power alone. You can imagine how sad this makes me. Do you want to do it? You don't have to do it. Your mother doesn't want you to do it. I want you to stay home and be safe. You are my only child."

Mangoshi looked at her father and touched him on the cheek and smiled.

"I will do it, Daddy. I have to do it. I feel as if something has been calling me to do it and I have not been listening."

"But you don't have to," said her father.

"Yes, I do. I must help save Mum. We must save the village."

"Are you sure?"

"Yes, Daddy. I think I'm ready."

At these words her father brightened. He gave
her food that her mother had prepared from her
sick bed. There was some bread, some fruit, and
a special cup for drinking water. He also gave
her a white handkerchief that had been tied into
a knot.

"Inside this handkerchief," he said, "there
are seven seeds. They are very small. They are
smaller than the eye can see."

"What are they for?"

"You have to discover that for yourself. Now
go and say goodbye to your mother."

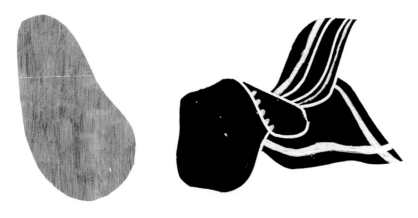

Mangoshi went to the room where her mother lay. She was fast asleep. Mangoshi watched her mother sleeping. She had grown very thin. The village doctor said she did not have long to live. Mangoshi began to weep for her mother and got up to leave. But her mother woke up then and called her back. She was too weak to talk, but she managed a whisper.

"So, you're going?"

"Yes."

"Don't go. It could be dangerous."

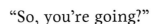

"I am only going to the forest nearby. It's not far. I will be back this evening."

Her mother gave her a strange look. Her voice was very weak when she spoke next.

"When I was your age, something called me and asked for my help. But I did not go. I did not help. We were warned against things like that. Then all my life things called me and asked for my help and I did not go. I was looking after my family. Now I am dying and something has called you, and you are going just like that. Why?"

"I don't know," Mangoshi said. "I love you, Mum. I want you to get better."

Her mother smiled.

"Do you remember the story of the hunter I told you some time ago?"

"Yes."

"You will be wiser than that hunter. Sometimes a short journey takes the longest time. I will be praying for you every step of the way."

Then her mother fell back into the sleep of the very ill. Mangoshi went out to her father, who was waiting for her.

"One last thing," her father said, as he walked her to the edge of the village, "the most important thing you have to do is to let the earth guide you."

"Thank you, Daddy. Please don't worry. I'll be back this evening."

With that the brave girl, with little footsteps, went out of the village and into the forest. She walked a short way and turned and waved to her father. Then she went on and when she turned back she could not see her father or the village anymore.

She thought she was walking into the forest but she was really walking though dry, scraggly trees. The land was burnt, trees were fallen, and there were no bushes for long distances all around. At first she was surprised at what she saw: the dryness, the ash of vines, the broken earth. Trees had been uprooted, and many had been cut and their broken trunks lay among their resplendent branches on cracked earth.

"What has happened here?" Mangoshi thought.

It seemed impossible to her that this was the same forest she had wandered through a year before. As she looked around she was dismayed and unhappy. Then she had the terrible feeling that she had come too late. At the same moment she realized that if the forest was not the same, she would not easily find the flower that would heal her mother.

She had a choice. She could go back. Her mother would surely die, and the villagers would die too. Then the forest would perish. Or she could carry on into what was left of the forest, till she found the trees that the special flower grew near.

She stood there, in the wrecked land, amid broken trees, their sap pouring into the earth, their branches scattered, and she saw that she didn't have a choice. What had happened to the forest would one day happen to the village. There was only one thing to do. She had to go forward and find that flower.

Mangoshi looked up at the sky. It was growing dark already. She had walked a long time. The destruction of the forest had been more extensive than anyone could have imagined. She walked and walked till she grew tired. She hadn't met anyone on the way. The forest was normally noisy with bird calls and

animal grunts and the fizzing of insects. But
now it was quiet. Then suddenly she felt in
the air a great suffering. She heard it first as a
terrible cry. She stopped and looked around and
could not see where the cry was coming from.
It sounded like a woman's cry. After waiting a
long moment, and not hearing the cry again, she
went on walking. But she did not go far. She was
hungry and she sat on a fallen tree and began to
eat the food her mother had prepared for her.

As she ate she heard someone weeping nearby.

"Who is it?" she asked, a little afraid.

There was silence in the fallen forest.

"Who is it? Don't be shy," she said.

"It's me," a broken voice said.

It came from beneath her. She leapt up from the fallen tree she was sitting on. It was an iroko.

"Why did it take you so long to come back to us? We had so much we wanted to tell you."

It took Mangoshi a moment to realize that the voice was coming from the fallen tree.

"Is it you talking to me, you tree that I have been sitting on?"

"Yes," said the tree, after a short pause. "Why did you take so long? We called you but you didn't heed us."

"I'm sorry," said Mangoshi. "I wasn't ready."

"It's too late now," said the fallen tree.

"It can't be too late. You're still talking."

"I'm at the end."

"How can you talk if you've fallen? I thought when trees fell they were dead."

"We take a long time to die," said the

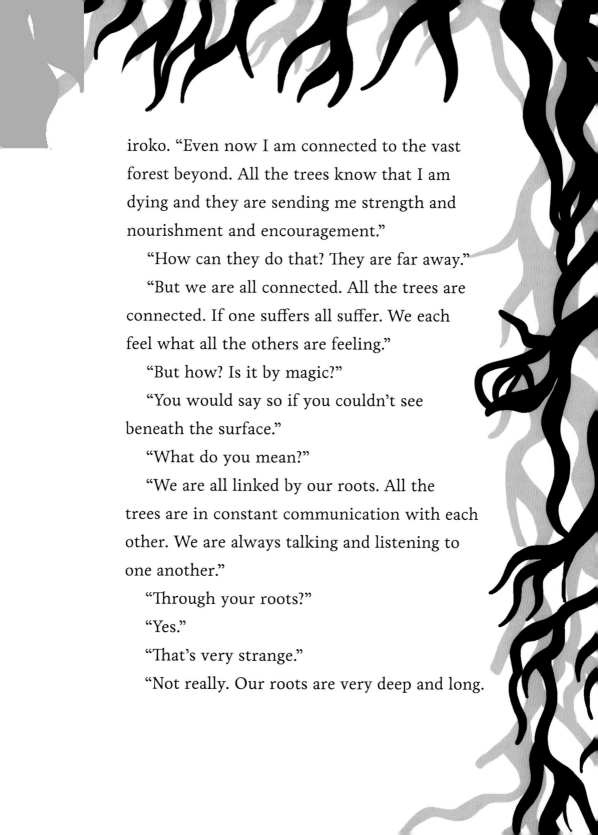

iroko. "Even now I am connected to the vast forest beyond. All the trees know that I am dying and they are sending me strength and nourishment and encouragement."

"How can they do that? They are far away."

"But we are all connected. All the trees are connected. If one suffers all suffer. We each feel what all the others are feeling."

"But how? Is it by magic?"

"You would say so if you couldn't see beneath the surface."

"What do you mean?"

"We are all linked by our roots. All the trees are in constant communication with each other. We are always talking and listening to one another."

"Through your roots?"

"Yes."

"That's very strange."

"Not really. Our roots are very deep and long.

Beneath the earth there is a whole
universe of linking roots. If you
think a forest is impressive,
even more so is the
world beneath
the earth."

"You don't sound like you're dying."

"That is because of the support I'm getting. Also, though I am fallen, I might still be able to grow."

"Can I help?" said Mangoshi.

"Yes, you can. That's why we've been waiting for you."

"How can I help?"

"You can help me later. But if you really want to help now you must travel on to what is left of the forest. Keep on going. It might be too late, but who knows."

"Are you sure I can't help you now?"

"The whole forest needs more help than me

right now. I will hang on. Go into the forest. The trees there will tell you what you need to know."

"I'll do that."

"But before you go," said the iroko, "tell me why you came back. Why are you here now?"

"My mother is ill. The village is sick. I have been sent to bring back a special flower that will heal my people."

"I know the flower you want. Your people have destroyed the forest so much that I am not sure you can find it anymore. It grows in special places and is very

rare. Only when the forest is healthy and happy does it grow. It can never grow when a forest is in trouble."

"What shall I do?"

"Go into the forest. Ask the oldest and the wisest tree for guidance. It's a baobab."

"And before I go," said Mangoshi, "tell me what happened to you. Why are you fallen?"

"Human beings came and cut me down."

"But why?"

"To sell me and make money."

"But if they do that there will be no forest left."

"I know. They don't know what terrible troubles they are causing."

"I'm sorry this has been done to you."

"Don't be sorry. Do something. Talk to the older trees. Go on into the forest."

"Thank you. I will."

Mangoshi put her arms awkwardly round the fallen tree.

"That's very nice," said the tree. "It will give me the strength to go on."

Then Mangoshi set off down the dry path towards the fading cloud of green in the distance. She walked for a long time past many fallen trees and she felt sad for them all. At last, when the sun was beginning to dip in the sky, she got to the beginnings of what was left of the forest. She walked on into its warmth. The air there smelt of bark and bushes. She heard animals cough not too far away. A few birds were busy up in the branches.

As she went deeper into the forest she heard a murmur of voices. It was low and steady and it rose and fell, like several people talking at once. Mangoshi had the feeling that the whole forest was watching her. When she looked she saw nothing but the mahogany and obeche trees and the bushes and the climbers and she heard rustling noises close by and up in the branches. She went on walking. The murmurs grew louder. And at last, very tired now, Mangoshi chose a mound to sit on and rest. She looked around at the roots of the trees for any signs of the special flower she had been sent to pick. She saw nothing but strangely colored mushrooms and the sloughed skin of a snake.

She was very tired and dozed for a moment.

The obeche near her bent its branches low and said:

"So you have come at last."

"Let her sleep," a sycamore said.

"How can she sleep at a time like this?"

"Leave her alone. She doesn't know what is happening yet or what is to come."

"But she must know. She is the only one who can tell the others before it really is too late."

"But is she ready?"

"She's here now. That means she's ready."

"Who will tell her?"

"I will," said the deep voice of an elderly tree.

"I heard all that," said Mangoshi, lifting up her head. "What is it you are going to tell me? I'm here now, and I'm ready."

"Why are you here?" asked the elderly baobab.

Like before, the trees had moved. They had

gathered round her, lowering their branches to
get a good look at her.

"She's very small," murmured a palm tree.

"How can she help? She's too small to help,"
said a conifer.

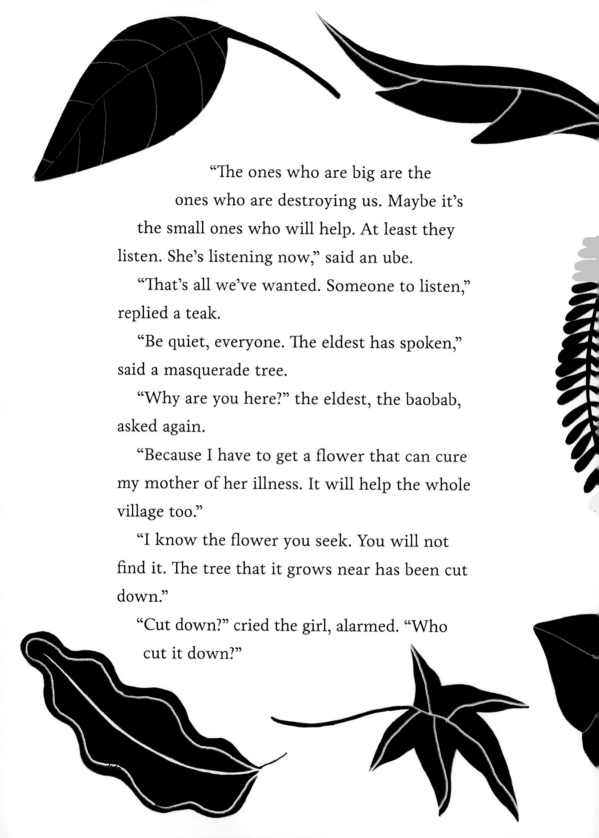

"The ones who are big are the
ones who are destroying us. Maybe it's
the small ones who will help. At least they
listen. She's listening now," said an ube.

"That's all we've wanted. Someone to listen,"
replied a teak.

"Be quiet, everyone. The eldest has spoken,"
said a masquerade tree.

"Why are you here?" the eldest, the baobab,
asked again.

"Because I have to get a flower that can cure
my mother of her illness. It will help the whole
village too."

"I know the flower you seek. You will not
find it. The tree that it grows near has been cut
down."

"Cut down?" cried the girl, alarmed. "Who
cut it down?"

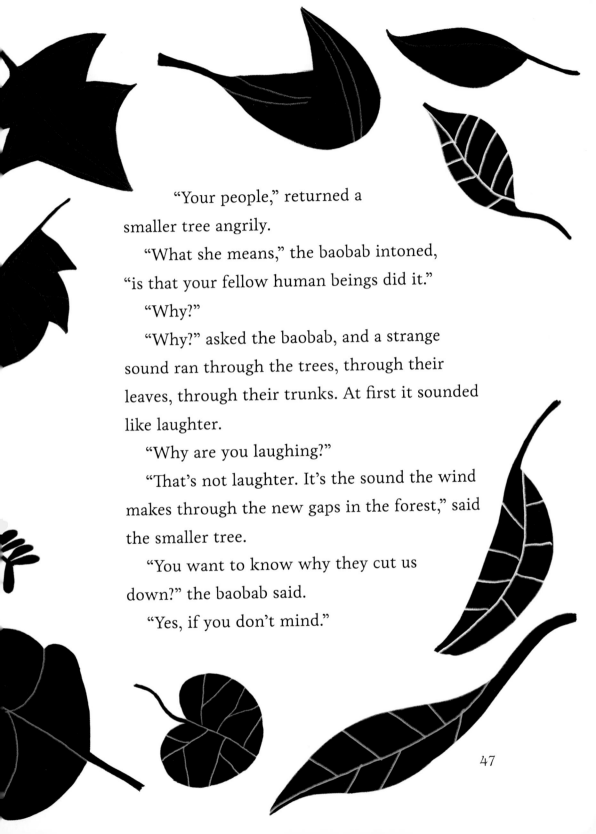

"Your people," returned a smaller tree angrily.

"What she means," the baobab intoned, "is that your fellow human beings did it."

"Why?"

"Why?" asked the baobab, and a strange sound ran through the trees, through their leaves, through their trunks. At first it sounded like laughter.

"Why are you laughing?"

"That's not laughter. It's the sound the wind makes through the new gaps in the forest," said the smaller tree.

"You want to know why they cut us down?" the baobab said.

"Yes, if you don't mind."

"Before we tell you why they cut us down, perhaps we should tell you who we are."

"I thought you were trees."

"But do you know what trees are?"

Mangoshi looked round, at the palms, the irokos, the obeches, the baobabs, the squat trees, the tall ones, the gnarled ones. She thought she knew what trees were. Now she was not so sure.

"What are you?"

"To answer that question we have to take you on a journey round the world and through time."

"But how?"

"It's very simple. Surrender yourself to the dream, and hold on to me."

Mangoshi put her arms around the babobab. She shut her eyes and surrendered herself to the great tree. Suddenly she was soaring through space. She was soaring above the branches and she saw before her, spreading as far as it was possible to see, a universe of trees. They were all bright and magical.

"We are not just trees," came the voice of the baobab, "we hold the earth together. We are the link between heaven and earth. We give the earth the air that humans breathe. We make the environment stable. We have great healing powers. We are older than the human race."

Then Mangoshi felt herself being taken below the earth, where she saw roots and branches of roots, linking and connecting one another beneath the wide earth.

"What is that?"

"These are our roots. Through these, trees talk to one another, share information, and even sense the future."

"What else do they do?"

"They keep us alive. Sometimes a tree looks like it is finished,

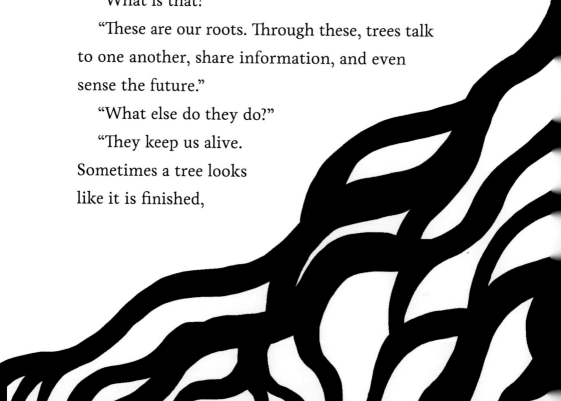

but so long as the roots are alive it can still grow.
Underneath the earth is where the real stuff
happens. It's a whole world down here.
You can travel from one end of a country to
another just through the network of roots."

"I didn't know a tree was so amazing."

"Take me, for example. Every part of me
is useful. My leaves and bark produce healing
medicine. My fruits are nutritious. My roots cure
many known and unknown diseases. My shade
gives peace and repels evil. A tree is just like a
human, you know. We are each very different.
Have you not sensed it, how we each have
our own unique character?"

"Yes, I have. Where are you
taking me now?"

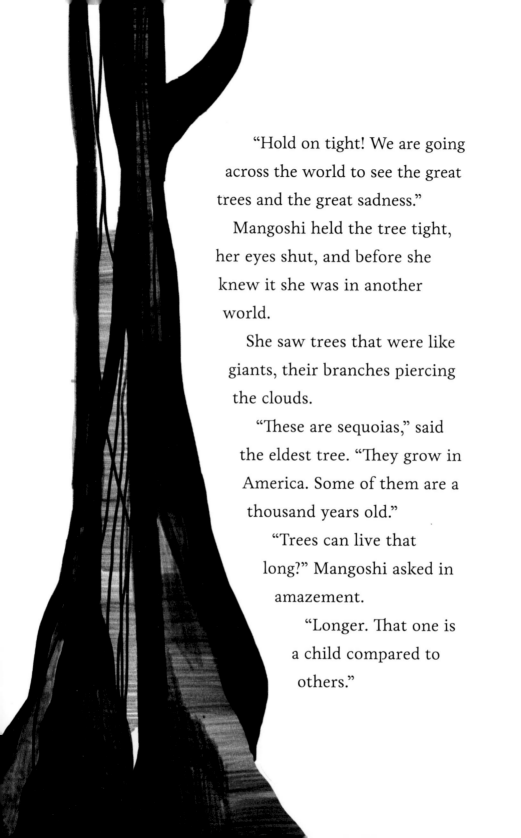

"Hold on tight! We are going across the world to see the great trees and the great sadness."

Mangoshi held the tree tight, her eyes shut, and before she knew it she was in another world.

She saw trees that were like giants, their branches piercing the clouds.

"These are sequoias," said the eldest tree. "They grow in America. Some of them are a thousand years old."

"Trees can live that long?" Mangoshi asked in amazement.

"Longer. That one is a child compared to others."

Then she found herself in the presence of the
oldest tree in the world. It was a bristlecone
pine. She expected it to be bent and scrawny.
It was nearly ten thousand years old, but it was
wild and robust, like a twisting dancer.

"How is it you are so old and look so strong?"
she asked.

"I am far away from people and their cities.
My thoughts are pure and my needs are simple.
I take each day as it comes.
If I have one secret it
is this. Around my
five thousandth
year I discovered
that time does
not really exist."

Then Mangoshi was taken to a place where the weather was cool. She saw massive trees with wide trunks and spreading branches.

"They are beautiful. What are they?"

"These are English oaks. They are very special. They used to be worshipped in the old days."

Then she was taken to a warm land and saw trees that were very broad and squat whose branches plunged back into the earth and seemed to become roots. Then she saw forests of trees all whispering, all aware of her.

"Where are you from?" the trees asked.

"From Africa," she replied.

"And how are the forests there? Is it true what we hear, that they are being cut down?"

"Yes," said Mangoshi.

The trees bowed their heads in silence. Then next Mangoshi was taken to a very hot place. There was sand everywhere. The sand was hot and the wind was hot and everywhere she looked there was only sand.

"What is this place?" Mangoshi asked.

"This is a desert. There is nothing here but sand. It is very hot. Nothing lives here. There are no trees." The baobab gave a low laugh. "There used to be extensive forests here."

"What happened to them?"

"The same thing that happens when they kill the trees."

"There are no people here either."

"I know," said the eldest tree. "How can people live where there are no trees?"

Then Mangoshi was taken far away to a huge
forest. But it was not a normal forest. It was
a place of great sadness. Trees were wailing
constantly. Mangoshi thought it was a forest
because at first she saw trees. But they were
not trees.

"What are they?" she asked.

"This is the Amazon, the biggest tree
graveyard in the world. Many years ago this
place had forests so vast that they filled a
continent. They helped the earth to survive. But
they have been burning and cutting down the
trees at such a terrible rate that there is almost
no forest left."

"But what am I seeing then if not trees?"

"These are the ghosts of trees. They are sad not
only because of what people are doing
to them but because of what will
happen to the world."

"What will happen to the world?"

"The trees give the world the air that we breathe. The more people destroy them the less air there will be for the world. Do you know what will happen if there are no trees in the world?"

"What will happen?"

"There will be no human beings."

"Really?"

"Yes, human beings need trees. When they cut down forests they are cutting down your future."

"It's terrible! Do people not know?"

"They can't know," said the eldest tree, "or they would not be doing what they are doing."

Mangoshi looked at the expanse of tree stumps. It was really the saddest thing she had ever seen. She could hear the trees weeping.

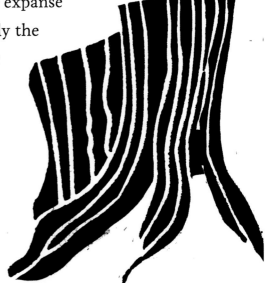

"Take me away from this place," she said. "This is too sad."

"I just wanted you to see with your own eyes what people are doing. Now come with me. Hold on tight."

"Where are we going now?"

But the baobab would not say. Mangoshi held on tight and was carried far across the world. She found herself in a strangely beautiful place. She saw a forest of small young trees. They were happy and singing.

"Where am I?"

"This is Africa. This place used to be a desert. It is one of the happiest places in the world for trees. We are making the desert live again. The people here have grown millions of trees."

"They look really happy. What makes them so happy?"

The eldest tree was silent for a long time. Then he spoke.

"You humans seem to think that we trees are just decoration. But we are beings

like you. We feel. We respond to love and attention. You should see how we glow when we are loved."

And in a flash the eldest tree took Mangoshi to the south of England, where there were ancient, rolling hills, and she saw these hundred-year-old ash trees. They were sky-reaching and their branches formed an immense canopy. They seemed to be enveloped in light.

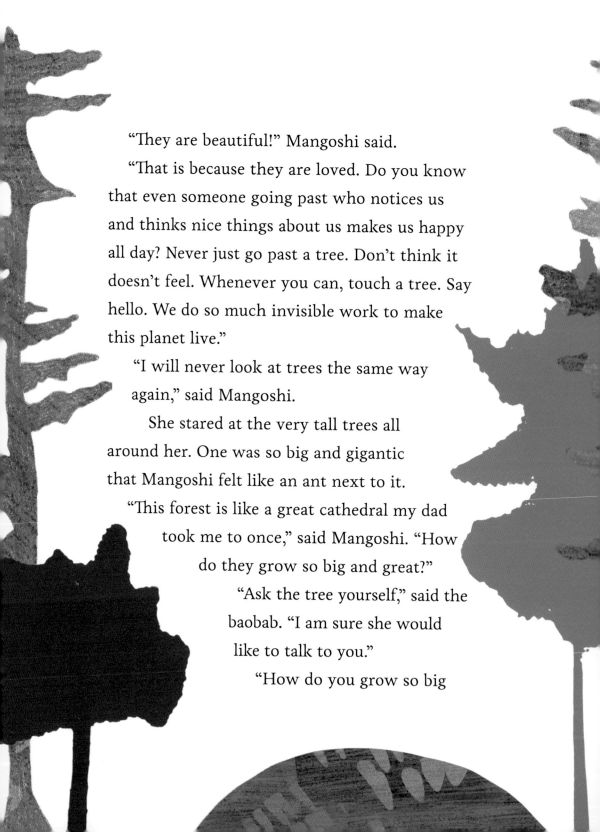

"They are beautiful!" Mangoshi said.

"That is because they are loved. Do you know that even someone going past who notices us and thinks nice things about us makes us happy all day? Never just go past a tree. Don't think it doesn't feel. Whenever you can, touch a tree. Say hello. We do so much invisible work to make this planet live."

"I will never look at trees the same way again," said Mangoshi.

She stared at the very tall trees all around her. One was so big and gigantic that Mangoshi felt like an ant next to it.

"This forest is like a great cathedral my dad took me to once," said Mangoshi. "How do they grow so big and great?"

"Ask the tree yourself," said the baobab. "I am sure she would like to talk to you."

"How do you grow so big

and great?" Mangoshi asked the big and great tree.

The tree gave a wonderful laugh.

"We started small, like most things," said the great tree, "and we draw love from the earth and draw love from the sun. We sink our roots deep into life. We support one another. None of us can grow great without the others. We don't compete. We help one another. We grow one day at a time. We have great patience. You will be surprised at the amazing things you can do with patience."

"I don't have enough patience," said Mangoshi. "My mum says that all the time."

"Patience is just another form of love," said the great tree.

"Love?"

"Patience is the love of life," said the great tree. "You love life so much that you don't mind taking time."

"But I want to do things quickly," said Mangoshi. "There's so much to do."

"We great trees take our time. We take all winter to grow one bud. We take half of spring to unfurl one leaf. We are in love with time. We watch the world hurrying around us, going nowhere. We take it slow, but we are busy all the time."

"Busy doing what?"

"Growing. Turning light into life."

"It's been lovely talking to you," said Mangoshi.

"Wherever you go, remember us. We trees do our work in silence, but without the work we do the world will fall apart."

"I will remember you always," said Mangoshi, and she gave the great tree a warm embrace.

There were so many places the baobab wanted to take her. There were so many extraordinary trees to meet. They met the dragon blood tree. It gave Mangoshi magical secrets of life that she wouldn't understand till much later. And they saw the anunuebe tree. It was very mysterious and sacred. The air whispered that everything that came near it died. They were making a brief visit to the Congo forests to see the afrormosia trees, whose crowns brush the clouds, when Mangoshi remembered her sick mother. Then she worried that she had been away too long.

"I have to go back home now,"
she said.

"Well, hold on tight!" said
the baobab.

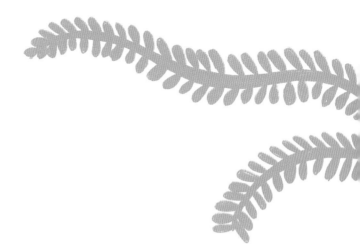

In a flash Mangoshi was back in the forest.
She woke up at the foot of the tree. Dawn was
beginning to show in the sky. It was quite cold.
She still hadn't found the flower. She stood up
and was about to go deeper into the forest when
she noticed the clearing all around her. The trees
that were there had gone. It was now an open
space. Then she saw all these large machines
standing around. And while she stared, men
came through the clearing with chainsaws and
machines.

"What are you doing here?" one of the men
shouted.

"I am looking for a flower for my mother who
is sick," said Mangoshi.

"Take her to the hospital. There are no flowers here," said the man.

"What are you doing?" Mangoshi asked.

"We've come to cut down this tree," he said, pointing at the baobab.

"Why do you want to cut it down? What has it done to you?"

"You're a child. You don't understand these things," said the man.

"I understand that you want to kill this tree for no good reason, and I won't let you," said Mangoshi.

The man laughed.

"What will you do? How will you stop us?" he wanted to know, still laughing.

"You will have to cut me down first before you touch this tree," said Mangoshi.

The man looked at her and ordered his workers to carry her away. The first man who touched her was so deafened by her screams

that he dropped her
and ran away. When
she screamed she
seemed twice as big.
The tree cutters did not
know what to do with
this strange child who
seemed to have doubled
in size and screamed
at them so piercingly
if they got close.

After a few minutes another man came over. He seemed to have more authority.

"What's going on here?" he said. "I'm the manager. We have work to do. You must go home."

"I'm not going. I will not let you kill this tree."

"Why not?" asked the manager.

"This tree is my friend."

The manager looked at the girl and at the tree.

"How can a tree be a friend? Do you know what we do with trees? We build houses with them, and furniture, and with some trees we make books. We have to do our work. Go home!"

"I will not go till you promise me you won't cut down this tree."

The manager looked at the tree and saw only a tree.

"I could call the police on you," he said, "but I won't. But tell me, why is this tree your friend?"

"He only wants to help us. He gives us air. All trees are our friends. They are good to us. Without them we will die."

The manager looked at Mangoshi.

"I have a daughter your age," he said. "I would be proud of her if she were as brave as you. So I will make you a promise. We will not cut down this tree."

"Nor any of the others. How would you like it if someone from the sky came and said they would save you but kill everyone else?" the girl asked.

The manager did not know how to answer the girl's question. By now the day was beginning to advance. It was getting hot and the men were restless. Somehow word got out of this strange event in the forest, where a little girl was holding up the work of tree cutters. A man from a newspaper came to witness it. He had a camera.

He was not the only one who came. People began to gather. They stood and watched the girl standing in front of the tree with her arms stretched out, as if protecting it from danger.

"What is she doing?" people wanted to know.

"She is stopping them cutting down that tree."

"Why?"

"She thinks that the forest protects us."

"She's right!" people said.

And more people gathered. The more people gathered, the more difficult it was for the tree cutters to do their work. The manager offered the girl money, but she would not take any. He threatened her. He said he would call the police and have her taken away, but she was not afraid.

"You are not going to kill my friend," she said.

The people who had come supported her. Children who lived in the area heard about what she was doing and came to join her. Some of their parents came too.

"What are you doing?" the children asked.

"Those people want to cut down the forest. I think we should stop them!"

The children liked the forest and could not understand why people wanted to cut it down.

"This tree is my friend," Mangoshi said.

The other children were charmed by this and they looked at the old baobab tree with wonder. The tree looked at them too, but did not speak. It kept quiet and was happy that the little children played around it. When Mangoshi was hungry she ate her mother's food and when thirsty the children fetched water for her in her mother's cup. The day passed and the tree cutters could not do their work because of Mangoshi and the children. Then they packed up and left for the day. The manager promised that he would bring big guard dogs the next day and it would be wise if Mangoshi was not around.

Evening fell and the other children left.

Most of those gathered went home. Mangoshi
remained there by herself.

It grew dark.

"It's brave of you to do this, you know," said
the baobab. "Thank you very much."

"You're my friend. We must help our friends,"
said Mangoshi.

"But you know,
you're the only one who
has cared enough to help us. There's
nothing we can do by ourselves. We talk
to human beings but they don't hear us."

"What do you want to tell us?"

"That terrible diseases will come if they
cut us down. Their lives depend on us. Only
human beings can defend us. That's why we are
grateful to you."

Mangoshi watched the night fall. She worried about her mother and the village. And she worried about the trees in the forest. During the night she could hear the trees murmuring. They were talking to one another. They knew they were going to be cut down the next day, when the sun rose.

"Farewell," said one palm tree to the others. "I have loved growing up with you all."

"Goodbye," said an iroko. "I am going to miss lifting my branches to the sun. I am going to miss talking to you all."

Then the trees started weeping. It was a very solemn sound. It was as if a church were full of people and all the people in it were sad because something terrible had happened and they couldn't stop crying. Mangoshi was sad with them and began weeping as well.

"So many of our brothers and sisters, so many of our friends have gone," said the baobab. "That's why we are so sad."

Mangoshi fell asleep while she wept. And in her dream she saw that all the trees in the world had gone. The world seemed empty. Then the people too began to disappear. She woke up in the morning with the sun. Then she saw the tree cutters. They had come early. They had come in large numbers and they had even more machines and equipment. When Mangoshi saw them her heart sank.

"Be brave," the eldest tree said to her. "Stand firm. Never show fear. You are small, but your very smallness is powerful. We will stand behind you, to give you strength."

Mangoshi looked behind her and it seemed to her that the trees had clustered closer. They seemed a big dense mass. For the first time she realized that trees could be angry. The trees of the forest were angry and in a strange way it showed.

The manager set his men to working but as they approached what was left of the forest something seemed to stop them. The forest seemed darker and thicker than ever before. Only Mangoshi stood between them and the trees.

"You will not touch a single tree in this forest!" Mangoshi said, in the strong voice of a little girl.

"What will you do, if we do?" said the

manager. He was very amused.

Mangoshi did not know what she would do. But she thought quickly.

"I will tell the world about it," she said.

"The world does not care," the manager said. "They have all cut down their own forests. Where do you think we are sending the wood from these trees?"

Mangoshi was speechless.

"I cannot give up," she thought to herself. "I refuse to give up."

The manager and the men began marching into the forest. They brushed Mangoshi aside, and she fell to the ground. But suddenly the journalist who had been there the day before appeared again. Behind him was a big group of people. They looked important.

"Who are you?" Mangoshi asked, with tears in her eyes.

"We have come to help you," said the journalist. "The story of your struggle is in all the newspapers. People are angry about the forest." The manager of the tree cutters saw the crowd and came over. One of the important women with the journalist spoke to the manager.

"I am the governor of this state. We want you to stop work on this forest."

"But you ordered it," the manager said.

"Now we want you to stop," the governor said. "The people are protesting about the forest. Stop all work for now."

The manager was very surprised by this turn of events. He and his men were forced to stop work on the forest. When they left, the journalist took pictures of the girl with the governor of the state, and pictures of the girl and her friend, the baobab. Then the governor and the journalist left.

By now it was early in the afternoon, when the day is hottest and the forest has a nice sleep. Now that they were not going to be cut down the trees were sleeping happily in their own shade.

Mangoshi knew it was time to go home. But before she left she said goodbye to her friend, the old baobab tree.

The baobab was smiling.

"Why are you smiling?" Mangoshi asked.

"Because if they had cut me down you wouldn't have seen this," said the old tree.

At its roots Mangoshi saw the special flower that was needed to save her mother and the village.

"Did you have it all along?" Mangoshi asked.

The tree gave a big happy laugh.

"It is a flower that only grows," said the old baobab tree, "when someone has made a great act of courage."

Mangoshi bent down.

"Oh, you special flower," she said, "I hope you don't mind my plucking you. But my mother needs you so she can be well again."

"I don't mind," the flower said.

Then she plucked the flower and made her way home. On her way back she became very hungry and she remembered the seven seeds in her pocket. She had thought that they were magic seeds to eat when she was hungry.

But as she made her way through the fallen trees of the forest, she realized that they were magic seeds to be planted, to make the forest new again. So she planted the seeds in seven places.

Then, carefully, she carried the flower back to the village. Her parents were overjoyed to see her. They were even more amazed that she had brought back the flower. No one had achieved that in a long time. Her mother recovered and the village was saved from the illness.

At an important meeting of the elders, this is what she said:

"The trees are guardians. It is because the forest is being destroyed that all these bad things are happening to us."

After that the village took up the fight to save the forest and the magic flowers of healing that it contained.

One night, as she slept, she found
herself in a place where the birds are
happy and the rivers are pure.

"What is this place?" she asked.

"This is a paradise of trees. Nothing dies
here. Everything lives in simple joy," said the
old baobab.

"Why did you bring me here?"

"For a little bit of peace you won't
find on earth. It is time to return to
your childhood."

Mangoshi went back to the forest often.

"Now I know what your secret is," she said
one day to her friend, the old baobab tree.

"What is it?"

"All the trees radiate love," said
Mangoshi, "and every leaf is a hallelujah."

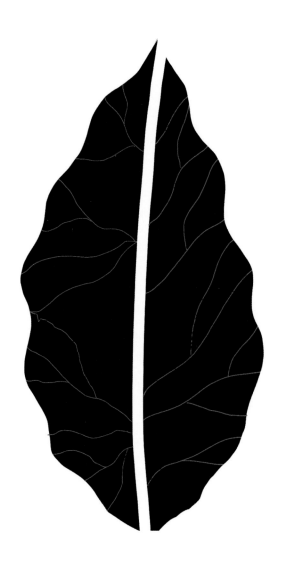

Ben Okri

Poet, Novelist, Playwright

Ben Okri is a poet, novelist, essayist, short story
writer, anthologist, aphorist, and playwright.
He has also written film scripts. His works have
won numerous national and international prizes,
including the Booker Prize for Fiction.

He has received many honorary doctorates
for his contribution to literature. His poem
responding to the Grenfell Tower fire of 2017,
read on Channel 4 News, has had over six
million views. In 2019 his novel *Astonishing the
Gods* was named as one of the BBC's 100 Novels
that Shaped Our World.

Diana Ejaita

Artist, Illustrator, Designer

Diana Ejaita is an artist, illustrator and textile designer who was born in Cremona, Italy, and now works in Berlin.

Her vibrant, dramatic work combines color and pattern in a unique way that magically reflects her Italian and Nigerian heritage.

"I love African culture," she says, "its literature, art and textile traditions."

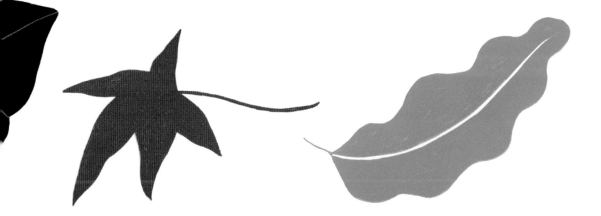